Come Along, Daisy!

JANE SIMMONS

Little, Brown and Company
BOSTON NEW YORK LONDON

To my mum
—J. S.

First published in Great Britain in 1997 by Orchard Books

First U.S. Edition

Library of Congress Cataloging-in-Publication Data

Simmons, Jane.
    Come along, Daisy! / Jane Simmons. — 1st U.S. ed.
      p.   cm.
    Summary: Daisy the duckling becomes so engrossed in
playing with dragonflies and lily pads that she temporarily
loses her mother.
    ISBN 0-316-79790-1
    [1. Ducks — Fiction.   2. Mother and child — Fiction.
3. Lost children — Fiction.]   I. Title.
PZ7.S59182Co 1998
[E] — dc21   97-26682

10 9 8 7 6

Printed in Singapore

"You must stay close, Daisy,"
said Mama Duck.
"I'll try," said Daisy.

But Daisy didn't.
"Come along, Daisy!"
called Mama Duck.

But Daisy was watching the fish.

"Come along, Daisy!" shouted
Mama Duck again.
But Daisy was far away,
chasing dragonflies.

"Come here, Daisy!" shouted Mama Duck.
But Daisy was bouncing on the lily pads.
Bouncy, bouncy, bouncy.
Bong, bong!

Plop! went a frog.
"Quack," said Daisy.
"Ribbit," said the frog.

Bong, plop!

Bong, plop!

Bong, plop!

Splash!

"Quack!" said Daisy, but
the frog had gone.
"Mama," called Daisy, but
Mama Duck had gone.
Daisy was all alone.

Bong, plop!

Splash!

"Quack!" said Daisy, but
the frog had gone.
"Mama," called Daisy, but
Mama Duck had gone.
Daisy was all alone.

Something big stirred underneath her.
Daisy shivered.

She scrambled up onto the riverbank.
Then something screeched in the sky
above!

. . . and closer,
and closer,
and
CLOSER . . .

It was Mama!
"Daisy, come along!" she said.
And Daisy did.

And even though Daisy played
with the butterflies . . .

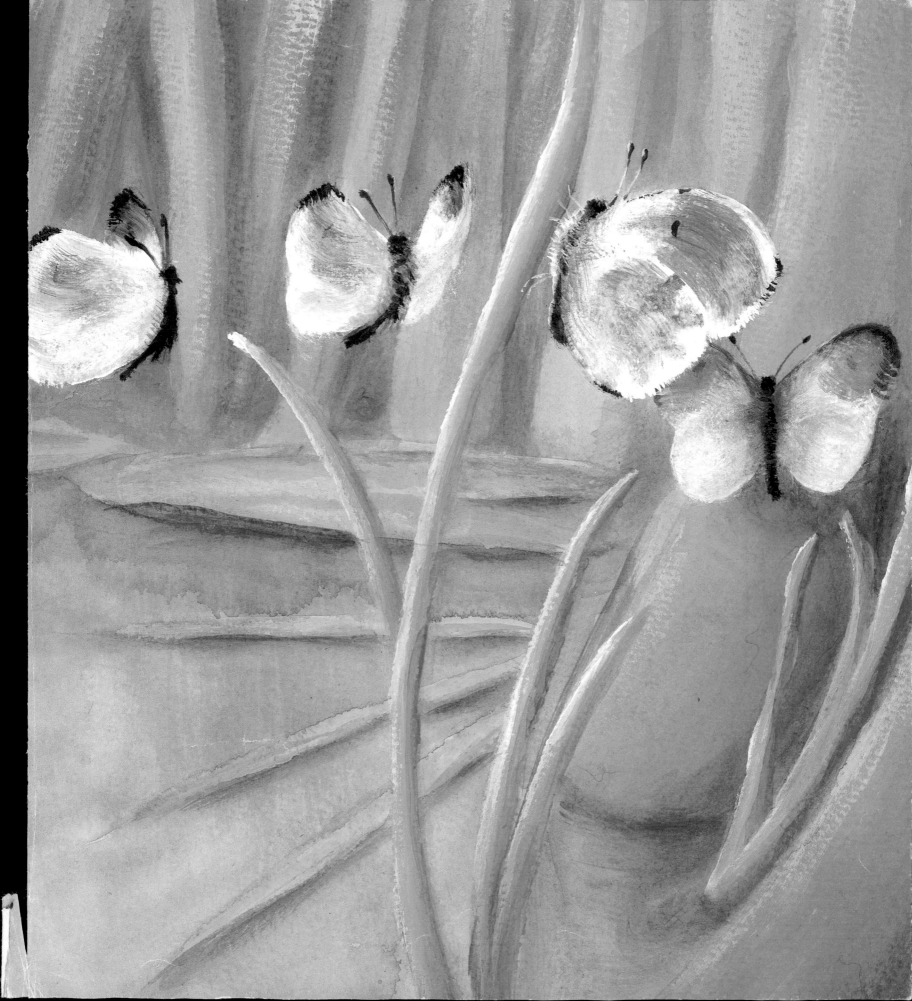

she stayed very close to Mama Duck.